WENDELL CROSS LIBRARY
1255 Hamilton Ave,
Waterbury, CT 06706

DRAGON MASTERS
FLIGHT OF THE MOON DRAGON

BY

TRACEY WEST

ILLUSTRATED BY

DAMIEN JONES

BRANCHES™

SCHOLASTIC INC.

DRAGON MASTERS

Read All the Books

TABLE OF CONTENTS

This book is dedicated to all the Dragon Masters
fans who write me letters and send me photos and pictures.
You make me smile every day! -TW

If you purchased this book without a cover, you should be aware that this book is stolen property.
It was reported as "unsold and destroyed" to the publisher, and neither the author nor the publisher
has received any payment for this "stripped book."

Text copyright © 2016 by Tracey West
Interior illustrations copyright © 2016 by Scholastic Inc.

All rights reserved. Published by Scholastic Inc., *Publishers since 1920.* SCHOLASTIC, BRANCHES,
and associated logos are trademarks and/or registered trademarks of Scholastic Inc.

The publisher does not have any control over and does not assume any responsibility for
author or third-party websites or their content.

No part of this publication may be reproduced, stored in a retrieval system, or transmitted in any form
or by any means, electronic, mechanical, photocopying, recording, or otherwise, without written
permission of the publisher. For information regarding permission, write to Scholastic Inc.,
Attention: Permissions Department, 557 Broadway, New York, NY 10012.

This book is a work of fiction. Names, characters, places, and incidents are either the product of the
author's imagination or are used fictitiously, and any resemblance to actual persons, living or dead,
business establishments, events, or locales is entirely coincidental.

Library of Congress Cataloging-in-Publication Data
Names: West, Tracey, 1965- author. Jones, Damien, illustrator. West, Tracey, 1965- Dragon Masters ; 6.
Title: Flight of the Moon Dragon / by Tracey West ; illustrated by Damien Jones.
Description: First edition. New York : Branches/Scholastic Inc., 2016.
Series: Dragon masters ; 6 Summary: The prime Dragon Stone seems to be dying, and that
means that the connection between the dragon masters and their dragons is also fading,
so the six dragon masters must locate the hidden stone, and learn what is causing the
problem before their telepathic connection is completely gone.
Identifiers: LCCN 2016019785 ISBN 9780545913928 (pbk.) ISBN 9780545913942 (hardcover)
Subjects: LCSH: Dragons—Juvenile fiction. Wizards—Juvenile fiction.
Magic—Juvenile fiction. Quests (Expeditions)—Juvenile fiction.
Adventure stories. CYAC: Dragons—Fiction. Wizards—Fiction.
Magic—Fiction. Adventure and adventurers—Fiction. GSAFD: Adventure fiction.
Classification: LCC PZ7.W51937 Fli 2016 DDC 813.54 [Fic]—
dc23 LC record available at https://lccn.loc.gov/2016019785

ISBN 978-0-545-91394-2 (hardcover) / ISBN 978-0-545-91392-8 (paperback)

10 9 8 7 6 5 4 3 2 1   16 17 18 19 20

Printed in China   38
First edition, October 2016
Illustrated by Damien Jones
Edited by Katie Carella
Book design by Jessica Meltzer

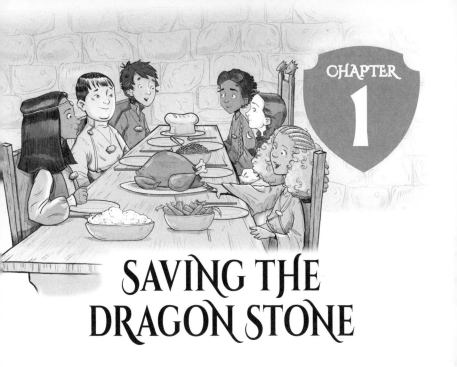

SAVING THE DRAGON STONE

I am really worried about the Dragon Stone," said Drake.

Six Dragon Masters sat around a dining table in King Roland's castle. Five of them lived in the castle: Drake, Bo, Rori, Ana, and Petra. Heru, the sixth Dragon Master, lived in the Land of Pyramids. The Dragon Stone had chosen each of them to connect with dragons.

Heru had flown a long way on Wati, his dragon. Wati was resting in the Dragon Caves. And Heru had brought important news — the prime Dragon Stone was dying!

"You are right to be worried, Drake," said Heru. "We must quickly find the prime stone so that we can try to save it. That is why I came here. My family thinks you and your friends can help us."

"Wait — what exactly is the *prime* Dragon Stone?" Bo asked.

Heru looked down. A green stone hung from a cord around his neck. Each of the others wore a stone just like it.

"We each wear a piece of the Dragon Stone to connect with our dragons," Heru explained. "All of our smaller stones come from the prime stone."

"So is the prime stone huge?" asked Ana, who was also from the Land of Pyramids.

"I think so," said Heru. "But I have never seen it. It has been kept inside a secret pyramid for many years. A scroll tells us that it will take six dragons to enter the pyramid. But first we must find it."

Just then, Griffith the wizard walked into the room.

"I have spoken with King Roland," he said. "I asked if you may all go to the Land of Pyramids. He will tell us soon. But I will stay here and look for a way to save the Dragon Stone."

"The king *has* to say yes!" said Rori. "If the Dragon Stone dies, we won't be able to connect with our dragons anymore."

Petra, the newest Dragon Master, turned to Heru. "If you've never seen the prime stone, then how do you know it is dying?" she asked.

"Our family has a larger piece of the stone, just like Griffith does," Heru explained. "Its glow keeps fading. And lately, I have  had trouble connecting with Wati. Those are signs that the prime stone is weakening."

As Heru spoke, Drake's own Dragon Stone started to flicker. It wasn't glowing strong like it usually did when Worm, his Earth Dragon, communicated with him. But still, Drake heard his dragon's voice inside his head.

Come! said Worm. *It is —*

Then his voice stopped.

"It's Worm!" Drake said. "It sounds like something is wrong, but he didn't finish his message. We must go to the caves!"

The Dragon Masters rushed down the long staircase that led to the Dragon Caves. Drake ran up to Worm, a brown dragon with tiny wings and a body like a snake.

"What's wrong?" Drake asked.

Worm nodded toward the cave of Vulcan, Rori's Fire Dragon. The dragon was snorting and pawing the ground.

"Vulcan!" Rori cried. She ran to him. "What's the matter?"

"His connection to you is getting weaker," Griffith explained. "Vulcan may be feeling confused and scared."

Rori reached through the bars of the cave and patted her dragon's nose. "Hang in there, Vulcan," she said. "We'll find a way to save the Dragon Stone!"

"Griffith!" Simon, a castle guard, said as he marched in. "King Roland agrees that the Dragon Masters should go to the Land of Pyramids. They may leave at once!"

THE DRAGON TEMPLE

Excellent!" Griffith said. "You are off to the Land of Pyramids!"

"My parents will be waiting for us when we arrive," said Heru.

"It sounds like a very long trip," said Petra. She twisted a blond curl around her finger. "Are we going to fly there?"

"No. We will have to use Worm's power to get us there quickly," explained Heru.

Ana's dark eyes shone with excitement. "Worm can get us there in the blink of an eye!" she said.

"Can Worm take *all* of us — and our dragons?" Petra asked.

Drake nodded. "First I'll tell him where to go. Then if everyone touches their dragon, and then touches Worm, he'll get us there."

"Everyone, please get your dragons ready," Griffith said.

The Dragon Masters
moved quickly.

Rori brought out Vulcan,
who was calmer now.

Ana led out her
shimmering white
Sun Dragon, Kepri.

Heru took out Wati,
a black Moon Dragon
who was Kepri's twin.

Bo's blue Water Dragon,
Shu, followed him out of
the cave.

Petra stepped
out with Zera, her
hydra — a four-headed
Poison Dragon.

Drake talked to Worm.

"Worm, can you take us to Heru's temple in the Land of Pyramids?" he asked.

Worm nodded, and Drake led him out of the cave.

"I will join you as soon as I can," Griffith told them all. "I trust that you will find the stone. And I hope that the key to saving it is somewhere in my books."

"All right, everybody!" Drake called out. "Touch your dragon, and then touch Worm."

The Dragon Masters obeyed.

Worm closed his eyes. His body started to glow. Then . . .

Whoosh! Green light exploded in the caves. When it faded, they weren't in the caves anymore.

They were outside. A bright moon shone on a stone temple. There were two dragon statues, one on each side of the door.

A man and a woman ran out of the temple.

"Heru! You are back!" said the woman.

"And you have brought help," said the man. "Very good. Welcome to the Land of Pyramids, Dragon Masters!"

"Everybody, this is Tarek, my dad, and Sarah, my mom," Heru said, introducing the Dragon Masters to his parents.

Then, six men wearing white tunics and pants rushed out of the temple.

"These workers will take your dragons inside," Tarek said. "We don't want curious villagers coming here. We have important work to do."

Sarah clapped her hands. "Come!" she said. "We must go to the temple's secret chamber!"

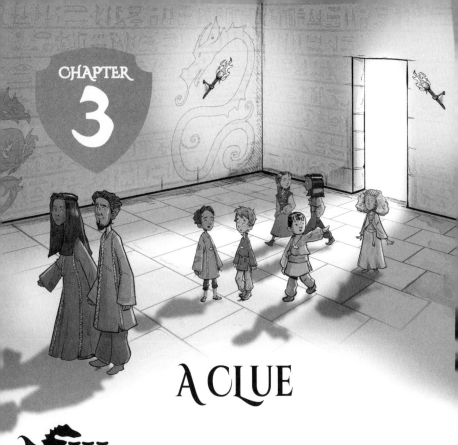

A CLUE

e are the keepers of the ancient secrets of the dragons," Tarek announced as the Dragon Masters walked through the temple. "These secrets have been passed down in our family for years."

Torches lit the halls of the temple. Pictures of dragons were carved into the walls.

They went downstairs and came to a room full of dragon statues. Sarah walked to a statue with sparkly green eyes.

"Those look like Dragon Stones!" Bo said.

Sarah smiled and removed one of the stones. The wall in front of her slid open.

She waved for everyone to follow her. The secret chamber was filled with shelves loaded with scrolls and books.

Sarah took one of the scrolls. She moved to a large table.

"This is all we know about the prime stone," she said, unrolling the scroll.

Drake looked at it. On top of the page was a strange-looking dragon symbol.

The rest of the page was filled with little pictures, not alphabet letters.

"This is very old writing," Ana explained. "In ancient times, people wrote messages with pictures instead of words."

"Yes," agreed Tarek. "I have read these pictures many times. The scroll says that the prime Dragon Stone is in the Pyramid of the Seven Dragons. But we do not know which pyramid that is — or how to find the Dragon Stone within the pyramid."

"There is also a rhyme," said Sarah. She picked up the scroll and read out loud.

A flying dragon will find the pyramid.
Six dragons are needed to find the prime stone.
Six dragons must go with their Dragon Masters.
No dragon or master can do it alone.

"The message is clear," said Tarek. "It will take six dragons to find the stone. That is why we need your help."

"One flying dragon to find the pyramid," Drake repeated. "Does that mean the pyramid can only be seen from the sky?"

Sarah nodded. "Heru has searched with Wati many times, but has not found the secret pyramid yet," she said.

"I will search again tonight," said Heru. "Wati can hold one more rider."

Drake's and Rori's hands shot up.

"I'll go!" they both said.

Heru grinned. "Drake beat you by one second, Rori."

"Yay!" cheered Drake.

Rori frowned. "Why can't we *all* fly with our dragons and look for the pyramid?" she asked.

"A dark dragon like Wati can fly at night without being seen," Tarek explained.

Heru turned to Drake. "Let's go find the Pyramid of the Seven Dragons!" he said.

"Good luck!" Ana called out.

WATI,
LOOK OUT!

rake ran outside with Heru. The temple
workers had brought Wati there. The boys
climbed onto the Moon Dragon's saddle.

Heru patted Wati's neck. "Wati, please fly
to the pyramids!"

Wati flapped his wings and took off into the air. The moon lit up the village below. The rows of houses gave way to the sands of the desert.

"We must look at all the pyramids from above," said Heru. "Keep an eye out for anything that could tell us which one is the Pyramid of the Seven Dragons."

Drake looked down. Dozens of pyramids were scattered across the sand. Three of them had pointy gold caps that glittered in the moonlight.

"Maybe it's one of the shiny ones," Drake suggested. "They look important."

Heru nodded and steered Wati toward the nearest one.

Drake looked at the pyramid closely. It had smooth stone sides and a golden tip. But nothing said that it was the Pyramid of the Seven Dragons.

"Wati, the next one!" Heru called out.

They flew to the second gold-tipped pyramid, and the third. But they all looked pretty much the same.

"These are not what we're looking for," said Heru.

They flew over more pyramids. They all had smooth stone walls.

Drake frowned. "I don't see anything special about these pyramids," he said.

"We must keep searching," said Heru.

Wati soared across the desert. He flew over another pyramid. Drake looked at it. The walls were smooth. Then . . .

"I see something!" Drake exclaimed. "That pyramid has squiggly lines carved into the stone. Do you see them?"

"Yes!" said Heru. "I did not notice them before. Wati, take us closer!"

Wati swooped down. He circled the pyramid.

Drake gasped.

There were dark lines on each side of the pyramid. Alone, they didn't look like anything. But when Wati and Drake circled the pyramid . . .

"It is the dragon symbol from the scroll!" Heru cried. "We have found the Pyramid of the Seven Dragons!"

Then Drake heard a rumble in the sky. He looked up. Dark clouds floated overhead.

"A storm is coming," he said. "We should get back."

"Wati, take us home," Heru said.

But Wati kept flying around the pyramid.

"Wati, stop!" Heru yelled. But the Moon Dragon didn't listen.

Heru looked down at his Dragon Stone. "My stone is flickering!" He gasped.

Boom! Thunder crashed. Lightning shot out of the storm cloud.

"We're flying right into the lightning!" Drake yelled.

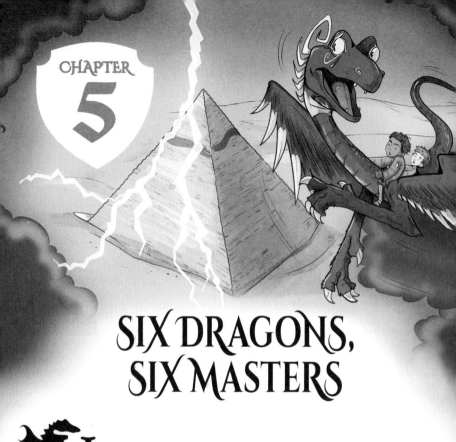

SIX DRAGONS, SIX MASTERS

Heru pulled tightly on Wati's neck to steer him away from a lightning bolt. Then the Moon Dragon flew back to the temple as a soft rain fell.

Drake and Heru climbed off Wati's back. Heru's parents and the other Dragon Masters ran up to meet them.

"Did you find the pyramid?" Rori asked.

"Yes," Drake replied. "But Wati became confused out there. Like Vulcan did back in the caves."

"My stone was flickering," explained Heru. "Wati couldn't follow my directions, and we almost got struck by lightning."

Tarek nodded. "We are glad that you are safe. Your connections with your dragons are really weakening now."

"It is good that you found the pyramid so quickly. There is no time to waste," added Sarah. "You must all go there at once to find the stone."

The other dragons were brought outside. The Dragon Masters touched their dragons. Then they touched Worm. Drake pictured the pyramid with the dragon symbol in his mind.

"Worm, take us there," he said.

Whoosh! In a flash, Worm took everyone to the Pyramid of the Seven Dragons.

Drake gazed at the tall pyramid in front of them. "Now we have to figure out how to get inside," he said.

"That looks like a door," said Ana, walking up to a big stone shaped like a rectangle.

Rori pushed on the stone. It didn't move. "How does it open?"

Petra studied the door. There were six symbols carved on it. "Maybe these are a clue," she said.

Drake looked at the symbols. He saw a
moon, a fire, a sun, and a drop of water. There
was a round symbol that looked like a rock.
And there was a skull.

"Wait a second," Drake said. "Those look
like..."

"... the powers of our dragons!" Rori said
with him.

Petra touched the skull. "That's the symbol
for poison. Maybe if I push on it, the door
will open?" She pushed on the skull. Nothing
happened.

"There are six symbols, and six of us," said Bo. "Maybe each of us needs to touch the symbol that matches our dragon."

He touched the water drop. Ana touched the sun. Heru touched the moon. Drake touched the rock. Rori touched the flame, and Petra touched the skull again.

All six stones pushed in. The door slid up.

"Hurry!" said Heru. "We must find the Dragon Stone and save it before it is too late!"

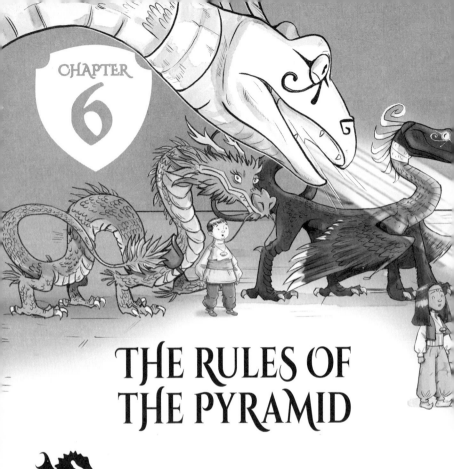

THE RULES OF THE PYRAMID

All six Dragon Masters and their dragons rushed into the pyramid. The door slammed down behind them.

"Kepri, light, please," said Ana. The Sun Dragon opened her mouth, and sunlight poured out.

Drake looked around. There was a large stone in the middle of the room. Words were carved into it.

Heru read them out loud.

INSIDE THESE WALLS ARE SIX SECRET ROOMS.
IN EACH ROOM IS A CLUE TO UNWIND.

CHOOSE ONE DRAGON TO SOLVE EACH PUZZLE,
THEN LEAVE DRAGON AND MASTER BEHIND.

THINK WITH CARE BEFORE EACH CHOICE IS MADE,
OR FOREVER YOU MAY BE CONFINED.

WHEN ONE DRAGON AND MASTER REMAIN,
THEN AT LAST THE PRIME STONE THEY WILL FIND.

"I just realized something odd," said Bo. "The rhyme calls for *six* dragons. But this pyramid is called the Pyramid of the *Seven* Dragons..."

"And why does it say we'll be confined?" Petra asked. "Does that mean we'll be trapped inside this pyramid?"

"It sure sounds that way," said Rori.

"Worm may be able to help us," said Heru.

"How?" Drake asked.

"My family studies all kinds of dragons," Heru replied. "Earth Dragon scales have power. If we each take a scale, Worm can transport us all out of here after one of us reaches the stone."

Drake looked at Worm. "Will that work?" he asked.

Drake's Dragon Stone began to glow. He heard the answer in his head. *It will work. You may take my scales.*

"Wait, how will we know when Worm is going to transport us?" Bo asked.

I will know when it is time to leave. Then I will tell the other dragons, Worm said.

"Worm will tell your dragons when it is time," Drake repeated. "Just stay close to your dragon."

He stroked Worm, looking for loose scales. He gently pulled out five scales and gave one to each Dragon Master.

"Thanks," said Rori. "Now what do we do?"

"I think the rhyme tells us what to do," said Bo. "Each of our dragons must have the power to get us out of one room and into the next."

Kepri shone her light around the room as the Dragon Masters looked for a way out. They saw four walls made up of stones — but no door.

"So which dragon gets us out of *this* room?" Ana asked.

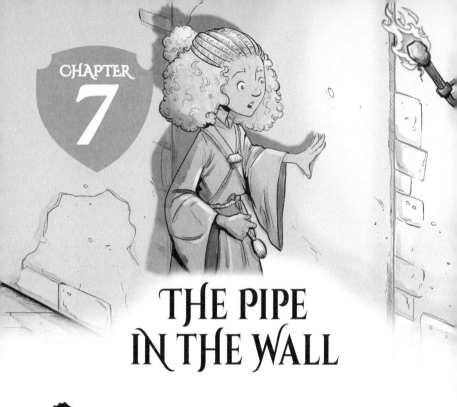

THE PIPE
IN THE WALL

I don't see a door anywhere," Rori said.

"We need to find the door to figure out which dragon can open it," Bo said.

Petra studied one wall. "What about this smooth area? There are smaller stones all around it."

Drake pushed on the smooth stone. It didn't move.

"This *could* be a way out," he said. "But there must be a special way to open it."

"I don't see any symbols this time," said Ana.

"Only one of our dragons can get us out of here," Heru said. "So, we must think about our dragons' powers. Which power could move this stone?"

"Vulcan is the strongest!" Rori bragged. "He could push right through it."

"I don't think that's a good idea," Ana said. "Remember that time when Vulcan tried to push through stone, and the tunnel collapsed on us?"

Petra looked up. "We don't want the whole pyramid falling on us!"

"I don't think Vulcan is the answer here," said Drake. He thought about when the tunnel collapsed. Worm had moved big rocks using the power of his mind.

"Worm can move stone," Drake said.

"Worm's powers could probably get us out of *any* room," said Petra. "So we might need to save him for something no other dragon can do."

Drake nodded. "Good point."

Bo was looking above the smooth door. A stone pipe was sticking out of the wall.

"Maybe that pipe is a clue?" guessed Bo. "Pipes carry water, and Shu is a Water Dragon..."

Drake understood. "Do you think Shu could shoot water into the pipe?"

"Yes, of course!" said Bo.

Drake felt a pang at the thought of leaving Bo behind first.

"You have Worm's scale, right?" he asked.

Bo nodded.

Drake took a deep breath. "Okay, so let's see if Shu can open this door."

Bo's Dragon Stone glowed. "Shu, please shoot water through that pipe."

Shu shot a stream of water right into the pipe. After a few seconds, the smooth part of the wall began to rise.

"It's working!" Rori cried.

The door stayed open as Shu continued to shoot water.

"Hurry, get through the door!" Drake yelled.

Everyone dashed through the door with their dragons. Drake looked back at Bo and Shu.

"We'll be fine!" Bo called out as Shu's water stream slowed down. "Good luck!"

Then the door slammed shut.

THE VINES

Kepri moved her head from side to side, shining sunlight around the second room. This time, the Dragon Masters and their dragons could clearly see the way out. A big round rock blocked an opening in the wall.

"Vulcan could try to push it," Rori said.

"First, we need to know more about what we're dealing with," said Petra.

Drake heard *drip, drip, drip*.

"Quiet, everyone!" he said. "Where's that sound coming from?"

Kepri shone light on a big stone pot set a few feet away from the big rock. The Dragon Masters crept closer to the pot. Vines were carved into the sides of the pot. Inside, the pot was filled with dirt.

Then Drake looked up.
A pipe stuck out from the
ceiling. It was dripping
water into the dirt.

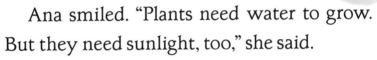

"This pipe must be
connected to the last
room!" said Drake.

Ana smiled. "Plants need water to grow.
But they need sunlight, too," she said.

"Of course!" said Petra.

Ana turned to Kepri. "Please shine your
light inside the pot," she said.

Golden light poured from the Sun Dragon's
mouth. It hit the dirt in the pot.

The dirt began to stir. A small green shoot
sprang up.

"It's working!" Rori cheered.

The green shoot grew into a thick vine. The vine grew out of the pot. More vines grew. They snaked away from Kepri, across the floor toward the big round rock. As they grew, they pushed the rock. They opened the doorway!

"That's good, Kepri," Ana said. The dragon stopped shining her light on the vines. But they kept growing — and they started to fill the opening of the door!

"We must hurry!" said Heru.

Drake, Rori, Petra, and Heru ran through the door with their dragons. The vines were growing bigger and bigger, and the Dragon Masters had to squeeze past them.

Drake looked back at Ana. He could see her and Kepri through the tangle of vines. Wati let out a sad cry.

Ana waved. "Keep going! We'll be okay!" she called out.

Then the vines closed off the doorway completely. Without Kepri's sunlight, the third room was very dark.

"Vulcan, fire," Rori said. Two flames danced out of Vulcan's nostrils. They cast a glow around the room.

The vines had chased them into this new room. They were growing fast! They spread out along the walls.

"I see a door! Get there before the vines block it!" Drake yelled, pointing to the far wall.

They raced across the room. But the vines reached the far wall before the Dragon Masters did. The big, thick vines blocked the door.

"We're trapped!" Petra cried.

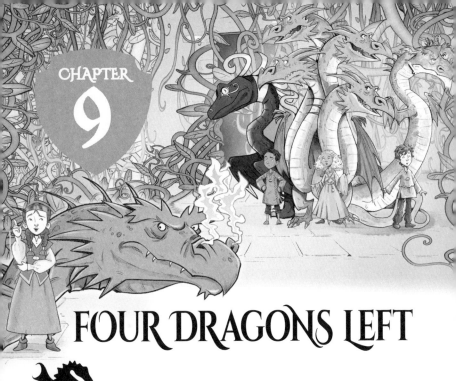

FOUR DRAGONS LEFT

rake tried to think fast. He looked around the third room. The vines covered every inch of the walls.

"Time for a bonfire!" said Rori. "Vulcan —"

"Wait, Rori!" Heru cried. "That could be dangerous. We have no way to put out a fire."

Rori's face turned pale. "I forgot we left Shu behind," she said.

"I have an idea!" said Petra. "Zera's poison can melt rocks. I bet it could kill these vines."

"Good thinking, Petra!" Drake cried.

"So I will ask her to spray the vines with poison where we saw the door," Petra said. "Then you can open it."

Heru nodded. "That's right."

Petra bit her lip. "What if Zera sprays somebody by mistake?" she asked.

Drake knew why she was worried. Zera's poison had accidentally hit both him and King Roland. It had made them very sick.

"We'll stay out of the way," he said. "Tell Zera to aim carefully. And make sure your stone is glowing."

Petra nodded. "Okay," she said. She looked down at her stone, which was glowing brightly. "Zera, aim straight ahead. Kill those vines!"

The hydra's four heads reared back. Liquid poison shot from each of her four mouths and sprayed the vines.

The vines withered and turned brown. They fell to the floor, and everyone could see the door again.

Rori ran to the door and easily pushed it open. "Let's go!" she called out.

Heru and Wati hurried after her. Drake followed, looking back at Petra. She waved to him with a brave smile on her face.

Petra and Zera. Ana and Kepri. Bo and Shu. All of them were trapped. Drake had promised that Worm would save them all. He looked down at his Dragon Stone.

I hope the prime stone doesn't die before Worm can get us all out! he thought.

FIRE!

Drake, Heru, and Rori looked around the fourth room. Vulcan's flames lit up the darkness. Drake could see lots of thick ropes hanging down from the high ceiling.

Then he spotted a door across the room. The door was made of a thin stone slab. A rope connected the door to a heavy stone cube that dangled above the floor. Another rope connected the cube to a metal loop sticking out of the wall.

"All right, this *must* be Vulcan's challenge," Rori said. "He needs to burn the rope that connects the cube to that metal loop, right?"

She pointed to the rope attached to the hanging cube.

"Good thinking!" Heru replied. "Then the cube will fall. And when it does, the door will lift up."

"Just be careful, Rori," Drake said. "Make sure Vulcan burns through only that one rope — or all those ropes on the ceiling will go up in flames."

Rori rolled her eyes. "You sound like Griffith," she said. "I am *so* good at controlling Vulcan now. I can ask him to make a big flame, or just a really tiny one."

Rori pointed. "Vulcan, burn that rope!" she cried. Her Dragon Stone glowed bright green at first, but then it flickered and went out.

Vulcan roared. He reared back. A fireball shot from his mouth!

The flames hit the ropes hanging above them. Within seconds, the ropes on the ceiling caught fire!

GLOW-IN-THE-DARK

Vulcan, no!" Rori yelled, shielding her eyes from the flames.

Heru hopped on Wati's back. He whispered to the dragon. Wati flew up and spread his wings, smothering the flames on the ceiling.

Wati flew back down.

"Good job, Wati!" said Heru.

"And look!" said Drake. "The rope attached to the cube wasn't hit."

Rori's Dragon Stone was glowing very brightly now.

"Rori, quick, ask Vulcan to try again!" Drake cried.

"But . . ." Rori looked scared.

"It wasn't your fault," Heru said. "Your stone was weak. But it is bright green now!"

Rori looked down at her stone. She patted her dragon's neck. "Try again, Vulcan," she said. "Just a small flame. On that rope. Over there."

This time, Vulcan hit the right spot. The flame burned through the rope. The cube-shaped stone dropped. The stone door lifted up. Drake, Heru, Wati, and Worm raced through it.

Then a spark hit the rope connecting the cube to the door. The rope burned quickly.

"Save that Dragon Stone!" Rori called after them as the door slammed shut.

The fifth room was very dark.

"Worm, can you glow?" Drake asked.

Worm glowed a faint green. Drake could see the outline of a door. There was a symbol of a crescent moon above it. But that was it.

"It looks like a Moon Dragon will have to open this door," Drake said.

Heru nodded. "Wati, moonlight, please."

A ribbon of dark light streamed from Wati's mouth. It looked like a rainbow made of blue, black, and purple. The light lit up the wall in front of them. Drake gasped.

Glowing pictures appeared on the door.

"The ancient writing didn't show under Worm's glow," said Drake. "Wati's moonlight made it show up!"

Heru read the message. "It says I must read the rhyme aloud to open the door," he said. "When it opens, you and Worm must pass through."

Drake's stomach flip-flopped. He suddenly realized he would be moving on alone. "I thought maybe *you* would be the last one," he said to Heru.

"You can do this, Drake," Heru told him. "Whatever you find in that room, you and Worm will handle. I have faith in both of you."

Drake looked at Worm. "Ready?" he asked.

Worm nodded.

Heru read the rhyme aloud.

A Water Dragon was dragon one.
Dragon two was of the sun.
Dragon three was poison green.
A Fire Dragon was fourth to be seen.
Dragon five was of the moon.
Will the Earth Dragon get them all out soon?

As Heru said the words, the door slid open. Drake and Worm entered the sixth room, and the door closed behind them . . .

A PUZZLE

Drake and Worm stood alone in the darkness.

"It's so dark in here," Drake whispered.

Worm's body began to glow with green light again. Drake could see six large stone balls in the center of the room, placed in a circle. They looked perfectly round and smooth. Beyond them, on the wall, was a stone door. Above it, carved into the stone, was a line of six holes.

"Do you think these stone balls go into those holes above the door, Worm?" Drake asked.

Drake heard Worm's voice in his head.

Yes.

Drake walked over to one of the stones. He put his arms around it. It was so heavy!

These are too heavy for me to move, thought Drake. *But Worm could move them with his mind.*

Drake looked at the stones. Each one had a symbol on it, just like the symbols on the front door. There was a moon, a sun, a water drop, a flame, a rock, and a skull.

Next, Drake looked at the holes above the door. He didn't see any symbols on them.

"How will I know which stone goes where? There must be a special way they need to go in . . ." Drake said.

Then he remembered the words from the rhyme that Heru had just read. "'A Water Dragon was dragon one,'" Drake repeated. "That's it! I bet the stones go into the wall in the same order as we crossed through this pyramid. So the stone with the water drop on it goes first. Ready, Worm?"

Worm nodded. The stone with the water drop glowed green. It floated up and . . .

. . . it fit perfectly in the first hole above the door.

"'Dragon two was of the sun,'" Drake said, remembering the rhyme. The stone with the sun symbol glowed. It floated up and slid into the second hole.

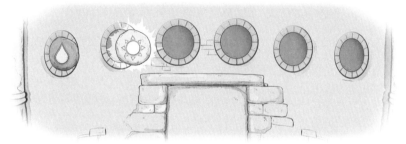

"Great job, Worm!" Drake said. "Zera was the third dragon, so the poison symbol is next."

Worm lifted the stone with the skull symbol. Then the stone with the flame. Then the stone with the moon.

"One more, Worm!" Drake cheered.

Worm's body glowed, and the stone with the rock symbol on it slowly rose up. It floated into the final hole above the door.

Creeaaaak! The door lifted up.

"We did it!" cheered Drake.

Worm crawled through the doorway with Drake. They entered the seventh room.

Suddenly, Worm sank to the ground! His glow faded.

"Worm!" Drake cried. "What's wrong?"

Worm didn't answer. Drake looked around the room.

There, towering above them, was the prime Dragon Stone. Light poured from the huge green stone, blinking on and off.

But the Dragon Stone was not the only thing in the room.

On the floor next to it was a golden egg! The egg was as big as Drake. Sparks sizzled and jumped all around it.

"Whoa! What kind of egg is that?" Drake asked.

THE PRIME DRAGON STONE

rake looked the egg up and down. The egg looked ... alive. Golden lightning bolts of energy shot out of it.

The prime Dragon Stone was pale green now. Drake could tell it was weaker than ever. Then he noticed that a stream of green light sizzled between the Dragon Stone and the egg. It connected them. And as the stone got dimmer, the egg got brighter.

"It looks like this egg is taking energy from the Dragon Stone," Drake said. He looked at Worm. A stream of green light flowed between Worm and the egg! The egg was taking energy from Worm, too.

What am I supposed to do now? Drake wondered. *We came so far to find the Dragon Stone. Now it's my job to save it.*

"But I don't know how!" Drake said out loud. "And even if I did, how will we get out of here if Worm has no energy?"

Think, Drake, think, he told himself. The egg was taking energy from the Dragon Stone and Worm. So maybe all he had to do was move the egg away from them to break the connection. Push it away.

But will I hurt the egg if I move it?

Drake took a careful step toward the egg. The hair on his arms stood up. The air was crackling with energy! He slowly moved his hand toward the egg, and felt the tips of his fingers tingle.

"Ow!" he yelled, pulling back his hand.

He couldn't push the egg. He might get hurt. If Worm had energy, he could transport it out. But —

Crack! Suddenly, the egg started to break apart. The lightning bolts of energy jumped toward Drake.

Worm's eyes shot open.

Worm's whole body glowed bright green. The Dragon Stone was glowing brightly, too.

Golden light from inside the egg filled the room. Worm quickly wrapped his body around Drake to protect him. Drake shielded his eyes. The light became brighter and brighter. It almost blinded Drake.

Whoosh! Worm and Drake disappeared from the pyramid.

LOOK! IN THE SKY!

Drake felt dizzy. He slowly realized that he and Worm were outside the pyramid — and all of his friends were, too. All of their Dragon Stones were glowing so brightly that the Dragon Masters couldn't look right at them.

"Worm got us out!" Rori cried.

"Good job, Worm!" Ana cheered.

"What happened in the last room?" Heru asked. "Did you save the stone?"

"I — I'm not sure," said Drake. "There was this egg, and it was taking energy from the prime Dragon Stone. Then it hatched in front of me and the stone glowed really bright —"

"Look!" Petra yelled.

Golden lightning bolts were shooting out of the side of the pyramid. Then a dragon flew right through the wall — like the wall wasn't there.

Bo's mouth dropped open. "What kind of dragon can slide through walls?"

"That must be what hatched from the egg!" Drake realized.

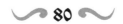

It wasn't a big dragon. It looked like a baby compared to the other dragons. Its scales were a shimmering gold color, and its whole body sparked with energy.

The dragon flew around wildly. It looked like it did not know which way to go.

"It's just a baby!" cried Ana.

Heru's eyes were wide. "That's a Lightning Dragon!" he said. "I have read about it in the scrolls. But I have never seen one."

Drake heard Worm inside his head.

We must help him.

"Worm says we have to help the dragon," repeated Drake.

"But what if he is dangerous?" said Bo. "Remember, he almost killed the Dragon Stone!"

Right at that moment, a bolt of lightning shot out from the confused baby dragon. It hit a palm tree and fried it!

Startled, the baby dragon let out a cry. Then he flew away across the night sky.

"No! Come back!" yelled Ana.

But the baby dragon was gone in a flash.

DRAGON ON THE LOOSE

The Dragon Masters and their dragons went back to the temple. Tarek and Sarah were waiting for them. Workers ran out to take the dragons.

"Our Dragon Stone glowed brightly a minute ago!" Tarek said. "You must have saved the prime stone!"

84

"We found the stone, but it didn't need our help after all," Drake said.

Ana frowned. "There was a baby dragon who needed our help, but he flew away."

"A baby *Lightning* Dragon!" said Heru.

Tarek and Sarah looked at each other.

"It sounds like you have quite a story to tell," Tarek said. "Let's get inside."

They went to the dining room of the temple. Sarah brought the tired Dragon Masters tea and little cakes dripping with honey.

Suddenly, there was a *poof* of smoke! Griffith appeared in the room with his wizard friend Diego.

"We have news!" said Griffith. "Tell them, Diego!"

"Every ten thousand years, the energy in the prime Dragon Stone creates a dragon made of energy," explained Diego. "It's called a Lightning Dragon, and its egg takes energy from the Dragon Stone."

"It's true!" said Drake. "I saw it happening!"

Then the Dragon Masters told their story.

"So the Dragon Stone *created* this dragon?" Rori asked.

Griffith nodded. "It looks that way. The Dragon Stone became weak because it was feeding energy to the egg. But now that the egg has hatched, the stone's powers should be strong again."

"At least for another ten thousand years," Petra added.

"That's why the pyramid is called the Pyramid of the Seven Dragons," said Bo. "The Lightning Dragon is the seventh dragon!"

Sarah nodded. "That makes sense."

"He's just a baby," Ana reminded everyone. "He's all alone out there, with no family."

"He must be afraid," said Bo.

"And he's shooting out energy like crazy," added Rori. "He could hurt somebody."

Heru frowned. "It will not be easy for a dragon like that to stay a secret."

Drake had another thought. "What if somebody bad gets the Lightning Dragon?" he asked.

Griffith stood up. "You are all correct. We must act fast to find this dragon and keep him safe," he said.

Drake looked at his friends. They had saved the Dragon Stone. Right now, he felt like they could tackle anything.

"We can do it," said Drake. "We will work together to find the Lighting Dragon!"

TRACEY WEST loves puzzles, riddles, and mysteries. She had fun creating the pyramid puzzles in this book, and she knew the Dragon Masters would know just how to solve them!

Tracey has written dozens of books for kids. She does her writing in the house she shares with her husband and three stepkids. She also has plenty of animal friends to keep her company. She has three dogs, seven chickens, and one cat, who sits on her desk when she writes! Thankfully, the cat does not weigh as much as a dragon.

DAMIEN JONES lives with his wife and son in Cornwall—the home of the legend of King Arthur. Cornwall even has its very own castle! On clear days you can see for miles from the top of the castle, making it the perfect lookout for dragons.

Damien has illustrated children's books. He has also animated films and television programs. He works in a studio surrounded by figures of mystical characters that keep an eye on him as he draws.

DRAGON MASTERS
FLIGHT OF THE MOON DRAGON

Questions and Activities

Why is the prime Dragon Stone important? What are the signs that it is weakening?

Why is Wati the **ONLY** dragon who can look for the Pyramid of the Seven Dragons?

How do the dragons use their powers to open the doors in the pyramid? Reread parts of the text to help you retell the information.

What was causing the prime Dragon Stone to weaken? Explain.

Write a narrative story about what **YOU** think will happen next with the Lightning Dragon! Make sure to use the words *first*, *then*, and *finally* to guide your story.

WENDELL CROSS LIBRARY
1255 Hamilton Ave,
Waterbury, CT 06706